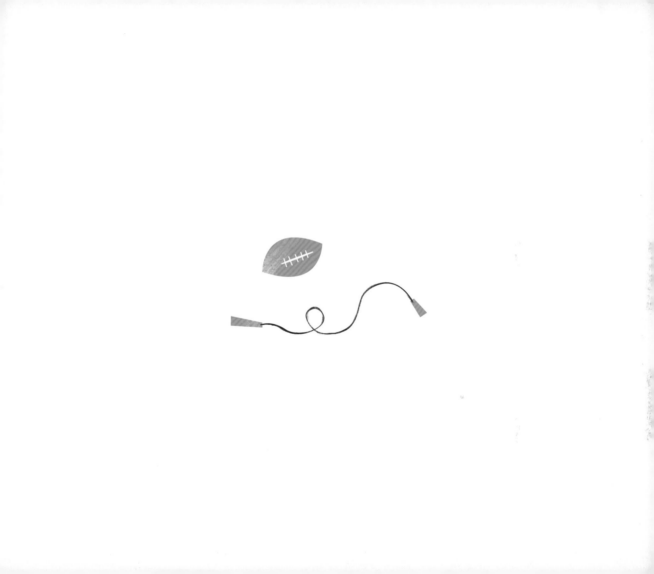

For Larry –E.W.

For Tracy, and all her patience –D.C.

Cover design © 2017 Deseret Book Company / Art direction: Richard Erickson / Book design: Destin Cox

Text © 2017 Emily Watts

Illustrations © 2017 Destin Cox

Library of Congress Cataloging-in-Publication Data

Names: Watts, Emily, author.

Title: Once there was a mom / Emily Watts.

Description: Salt Lake City, Utah : Deseret Book, [2017] | Summary: Once there was a mom who did so many things for her kids from morning until night that she almost forgot why she was doing it.

Identifiers: LCCN 2016048600 | ISBN 9781629723075 (hardbound : alk. paper)

Subjects: | CYAC: Mothers—Fiction. | Love—Fiction.

Classification: LCC PZ7.1.W417 On 2017 | DDC [E]—dc23

LC record available at https://lccn.loc.gov/2016048600

Printed in China   10/2016

RR Donnelley, Shenzhen, China

10 9 8 7 6 5 4 3 2 1

ONCE THERE WAS A MOM

Written by Emily Watts

Illustrated by Destin Cox

DESERET
BOOK

Salt Lake City, Utah

Once there was a mom...

...who had many beautiful children.

Actually, there were only two or three of them,
but sometimes that **FELT** like many.

The mom loved her children

So, So MUCH.

They were the stars in her sky,

the flowers in her garden,

the hot fudge on her ice cream.

They were also

the crayon on her walls,

the crumbs on her floor,

the dark circles under her eyes.

The mom loved to spend time
with her children.

But for such small people,
they certainly took up a lot of it.

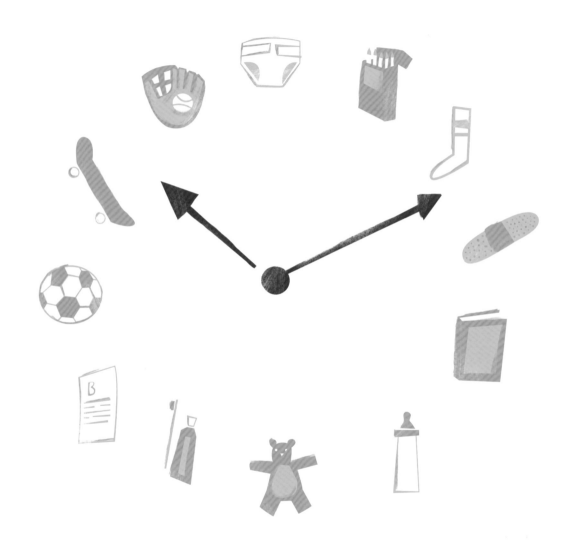

The
children
had
many
storybooks,
which
the
mom
loved
to
read
to
them.

"Again!" the children would cry.
"Again! Again!"

The mom had **MANY** stories memorized.

The children had many delightful toys.

The toys **FLASHED** and **BEEPED** and **SANG,**

and one of them made a noise
almost exactly like a real fire engine.

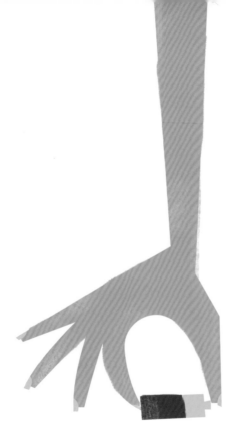

Sometimes the mom took the batteries
out of the toys to give them a rest.

The children loved to eat whatever
the mom fixed for them.

Mostly.

Nothing with green flecks.
Or unidentified bits that might be onions.
Or crusts.

The mom ate MANY leftover crusts.

At bedtime, the children would snuggle
into their cozy beds.

The mom would bring them one drink

and read them two stories

and sing them three lullabies

and pat them on the back ten times
to calm them down.

Sometimes they stayed in their beds all night.

And sometimes they didn't.

The mom loved her children with every bit of her heart.

But she was often very tired.

Sometimes the tired mom
would try to relax in a hot bath.

"Mom! Mom!"
the children would cry, pounding on the door.
"Let us in!"

Sometimes the tired mom would try
to restore her energy with a bite of chocolate.

"Mom! Mom!"
the children would beg, tugging on her arm.
"We want some!"

Sometimes the tired mom
would go out for the day.

"Mom! Mom!"
the children would squeal
when she got home.

"WE MISSED YOU!"

They would rush to hug her tight.

"Mom" was the biggest word in her world.

It made her want to dance,

and it made her want to hide.

And on some nights,
when the house was dark and still
and the moon peeked through the window,
it made her wonder.

Was it enough,

all those games of checkers and sheets of long division and birthday cakes and pushes on swings and shampooed heads and freshly washed jeans and trips to the dentist and Halloween costumes and plates of spaghetti and piano recitals and rides to school and a million other things that were so tiny they could hardly matter?

Thoughts swirled in the mom's head
like the moonlight swirling over
    the tiles on the floor,

        the books on the shelves,

            the folds in her blanket.

And suddenly,
there in the moonlight,
she had an epiphany!

Tile by tile, the floor had been laid.

Word by word, the books had been written.

Thread by thread, the blanket had been woven.

No one tile or one word or one thread
by itself meant much of anything...

The mom ran on tiptoe
to the children's bedroom.
She eased the door open
so she could see them sleeping.

"Bit by bit," she whispered,
"I am building a beautiful life for you."

And bit by bit, she realized,
they were making her life beautiful too.

Altogether, it was almost more beauty
than her heart could hold.

And all of the bits,
all of the love,
all of the joy stretching into the future
for her and her children
and her children's children—

it had all been set in motion because...

Once there was a mom.

EMILY WATTS

Emily Watts is the joyful mother of five children and grandmother of ten (so far). Her lifelong fascination with words led her to a career in editing. She has worked for more than thirty-five years in the publishing department at Deseret Book Company, working from home part-time for many of those years so she could be with her family. She is now executive editor at Deseret Book as well as a favorite Time Out for Women speaker and the author of several books, including *The Slow-Ripening Fruits of Mothering* and *I Hate It When Exercise Is the Answer: A Fitness Program for the Soul*. Emily and her husband, Larry, live in Taylorsville, Utah.

DESTIN COX

Destin Cox is a new dad excited for the day his daughter can hold a pencil so they can draw pictures together. His childhood focus on doodling in the margins rather than doing the homework on the page eventually landed him a career in design and illustration. He is currently a creative director for an ad agency. Destin grew up in Delaware, of all places, and loves his cheesesteaks and his Eagles. He now lives in Salt Lake City with his wonderful wife, Tracy, and their daughter, Prudence.